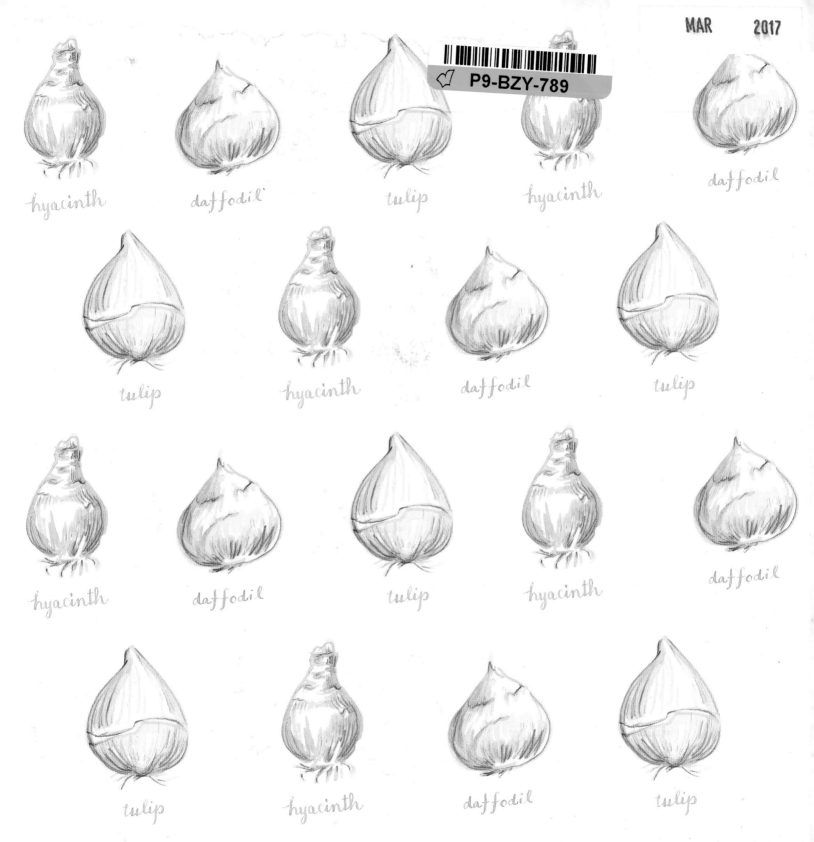

hyacinth daffodil tulip hyacinth daffodil

tulip hyacinth daffodil tulip

hyacinth daffodil tulip hyacinth daffodil

tulip hyacinth daffodil tulip

MAR 2017

Bloom

Deborah Diesen

Pictures by *Mary Lundquist*

FARRAR STRAUS GIROUX
NEW YORK

For my parents, Ron and Wilma Diesen,
with a big bouquet of love,
admiration, and gratitude —D.D.

For my family —M.L.

Farrar Straus Giroux Books for Young Readers
175 Fifth Avenue, New York 10010

Text copyright © 2017 by Deborah Diesen
Pictures copyright © 2017 by Mary Lundquist
All rights reserved
Color separations by Bright Arts (H.K.) Ltd.
Printed in China by Toppan Leefung Printing Ltd.,
Dongguan City, Guangdong Province
Designed by Roberta Pressel
First edition, 2017
10 9 8 7 6 5 4 3 2 1

mackids.com

Library of Congress Cataloging-in-Publication Data

Names: Diesen, Deborah, author. | Lundquist, Mary, illustrator.
Title: Bloom / Deborah Diesen ; pictures by Mary Lundquist.
Description: First edition. | New York : Farrar Straus Giroux, 2017. |
    Summary: A mother and child plant flower bulbs in the fall, wait through
    the winter, and see them bloom in the spring.
Identifiers: LCCN 2016001910 | ISBN 9780374302504 (hardback)
Subjects: | CYAC: Mother and child—Fiction. | Gardening—Fiction. |
    Seasons—Fiction. | Growth—Fiction. | BISAC: JUVENILE FICTION / Family /
    Parents. | JUVENILE FICTION / Concepts / Seasons. | JUVENILE FICTION /
    Nature & the Natural World / General (see also headings under Animals).
Classification: LCC PZ7.D57342 Bl 2017 | DDC [E]—dc23
LC record available at https://lccn.loc.gov/2016001910

Our books may be purchased in bulk for promotional, educational, or business
use. Please contact your local bookseller or the Macmillan Corporate and
Premium Sales Department at (800) 221-7945 ext. 5442 or by e-mail at
MacmillanSpecialMarkets@macmillan.com.

Do you remember when we planted those flower bulbs together?

One of us dug the holes while the other laughed
at the bulbs' funny shapes and crinkly skins.
Together we dropped the bulbs, one by one,
into their growing spots.

We held clumps of dirt in our palms and mashed them up, just to feel the rhythm of the bumpy soil in our hands.

We covered the holes with dirt.
We spread the dirt evenly.

The wind made the tree leaves dance, and one of us chased a beautiful orange leaf all across the yard. The other one watched—

and then joined in too, running through the rays of warm sunshine.

When we looked at the garden we'd planted
and thought about those bulbs, both of us
secretly wondered how something so small
could ever possibly grow big and tall.

Could ever possibly bloom!

In all the time that's
passed since then—

the doors we've
walked through,

the celebrations,

the big trip we took,

and even the time
that we cried—

so much has happened

that I'd almost forgotten
about the garden we planted.

But the bulbs did not forget.
Their roots pushed deep.
Their stems grew strong.

They heard the call of the sun.
They decided how to answer.

They grew steadily.
Surely.
Day by day, each day a bit bigger.
Stronger.
As certain as love.

And now, from those tiny little bulbs,
the ones that we planted together,
so long ago,

Just look . . .

at what has grown!

DAFFODIL   HYACINTH   TULIP   DAFFODIL   HYACINTH

TULIP   DAFFODIL   HYACINTH   TULIP   DAFFODIL

DAFFODIL   HYACINTH   TULIP   DAFFODIL   HYACINTH